Published By
DISTINCTLY D[...]
BOOKS AND P[...]
29 Dairy Close
London NW10 ___
www.distinctlydifferent.org

Copyright © Atiti Sosimi 2004
All Rights Reserved. This book, or parts thereof, may not be reproduced in any form without permission.

Printed and bound in Great Britain by Axis Europe PLC

A CIP catalogue record for this book is available from the British Library

ISBN 0-9543945-3-4

This book is sold subject to the condition that it shall not, by way of trade or otherwise, be lent re-sold, hired out, or otherwise circulated without the publisher's prior consent in any form of binding or cover other than that in which it is published and without a similar condition including this condition being imposed on the subsequent purchaser.

For more information about
THE BIG SECRET
Books, Learning Tools and Resources
0870 747 9841
www.the-big-secret.org

It's a secret And...

Shhh.....

MY LIPS ARE SEALED!

The BIG SECRET

FAMILY

This is a story about a young girl; she had an older sister and a baby brother. She was the middle child.

Her older sister was very clever and the young girl always felt she had to be as clever as her sister. Actually, her older sister was a 'bookworm' who hardly ever wanted to play.

Her younger brother was a lovely cute baby, but sadly he was too young to play games with her, so

she often found herself playing alone, making up games and **stories**.

These stories were so captivating that they seemed **REAL**.

Now this young girl had a **BIG SECRET**, it was so **BIG** a secret that she couldn't afford to let anyone know anything about it.

SCHOOL

At school she had two friends, one named Diane and the other named Francesca; but guess what?

They didn't know anything about the **BIG SECRET**.

The young girl wasn't a great fan of school, but she went there and did what she was supposed to do

As she moved up from infant school to junior school, so did her **BIG SECRET**. Yet even though she sometimes felt the secret was a little too **BIG** for her on her own, she kept it because it also excited her to think that she knew something no-one else knew.

Things didn't change an awful lot at home when she moved up into junior school; her older sister continued to be a bookworm and her younger brother grew up from being a cute baby into a cute toddler. In fact, the only thing that seemed to change was the size of her secret. It just kept on getting **BIGGER** and **BIGGER**.

The older she grew the **BIGGER** it got.

Suddenly, something changed at home. Her family decided to move abroad to live in a sunny warm country.

Her **BIG SECRET** moved too!

LIVING ABROAD

Soon she would start a new school, make new friends and the young girl was very excited.

Her older sister went first to sit the exams and was given a place in school straight away.

Then it was her turn. Her parents got her ready and she went for her exams; she was so excited.

Sadly, she wasn't as lucky as her sister and didn't do as well as she needed to do to get a place in her year, so she was given a place in a much lower class.

She didn't mind all that much because at least she had her secret and it was still safe ... although she was beginning to wonder ...

School abroad was very different and the work seemed much harder, although her older sister settled in well.

She also had something else on her mind ... her secret had become so **BIG** it was truly too much for her to manage alone and she didn't know what to do because she couldn't tell anyone. After all, it was a **BIG SECRET**.

She knew she was running out of time and sooner or later someone would get to know, so she tried to hide it. She tried everywhere, but alas ... there was nowhere she could

keep it safe anymore. She felt she'd better tell someone she could **trust** and then she wouldn't have to keep the **BIG SECRET** all to herself. And anyhow, she believed the **BIG SECRET** was responsible for a couple of close shaves she'd recently had.

IT'S TIME TO TELL

Now she'd decided to tell, she had the difficult job of deciding whom to tell.

Hmmm ...

Should I tell my brother?
No! He's too young ...
Should I tell my sister?
No! She's too serious ...
Should I tell my mummy?
Yes, but she's away for two weeks ...
Should I tell my daddy?
I guess so, because I trust him and if I were to tell my new friends, they could laugh at me ...

So she decided to tell her Daddy. That day as he came home from work, she went up to him and asked him if he could keep a secret.

He looked down at her over the rim of his glasses and said, "If you tell someone then it's not a secret anymore." She replied, somewhat desperately, "I know, but I've been keeping it all this time and it's just

got **BIGGER** and **BIGGER** and I don't feel I can keep it any longer and it's already got me into trouble.

Her father looked at her and said, "In that case **TELL IT**! Let's go and sit down and you can share this **BIG SECRET** with me."

He took her by the hand and they walked into the living room and sat on the settee.

She looked at her father, heaved a **BIG** sigh, looked down at her lap and blurted, "Well, the secret is …

PLEASE HELP ME.

Her father was dumbstruck!

Full of mixed emotions he babbled...
*"of course I will...
of course I will..."
he repeated in despair.*
.
*"Thank you so much for telling **me**
your **BIG SECRET**".*

This is a TRUE story.

At the age of eight, she shared the **BIG SECRET** with her father and, at thirty-eight, she shares it with you.

Why?

- To inspire you
- So that you realise that you can share the weight of the big secret
- So that you never feel limited by it
- So that, like the author, you will overcome it and be personally effective in your life, in your job, in all you do

But most importantly ...

- So that others will find the strength from your testimony to **TELL IT**!

Today the young girl in the story has a First Degree in Sociology, is a published Author, a Publisher, a Motivational Speaker, a Trainer and is married with six children.

As an adult, she realised that it was her dyslexia that had made simple things appear to be so insurmountable to her.

Nevertheless, somehow she had always managed to get by, mastering the art of telling stories without having to rely on written words because she paid apt attention to all the other details [pictures, shapes, sizes, colours etc] and used these details to tell the story. Whilst she did recognise some words, she perfected the skill of bluffing her way through tough situations.

All said and done, she slipped through the net.

Her lack of recognition of words, understanding of sentences / definitions and general inability to keep up with the expectations of her age group was always put down to laziness, not paying enough attention, not being careful enough with her work, but never down to the fact that maybe, just maybe, she needed some kind of specific support, teaching or … training.

Do you have a **BIG SECRET**?

Too many of us are hiding away with a **BIG SECRET** and no-one to share it with.

Worse still is the fact that **IT WILL** impact on your life and on your work.
Typically you will tailor your life around the secret, but like the young girl in the story you don't have to, you can do something about the **BIG SECRET**.

YOU can … **TELL IT**.

Personal message from AH-TT to all readers

Buy this book for a family member, a friend, a work colleague, or anyone who comes to mind as you read through this book. They will appreciate it more than you realise.

Remember... precious gifts come in small sizes and this tool of deliverance is a precious gift. This is why I have chosen to share it with you.

**Stay Strong!
AH-TT**

To Order A Copy

THE BIG SECRET

BY AH-TT

Call +44 870 747 9841
For more information about
THE BIG SECRET
Books, Learning Tools and Resources
+44 870 747 9841
www.the-big-secret.org

To order large quantities of this book for educational purposes employee training / giveaway, charitable and fundraising uses, etc. Please write and request a quote from the publishers:
**Distinctly Different Books & Publications Ltd,
29 Dairy Close, Willesden, London NW10 3RJ.**